American edition published in 2021
by New Frontier Publishing Europe Ltd
www.newfrontierpublishing.us

First published in the UK in 2020
by New Frontier Publishing Europe Ltd
Uncommon, 126 New King's Road, London SW6 4LZ, United Kingdom
www.newfrontierpublishing.co.uk

ISBN: 978-1-913639-16-7

Distributed in the United States and Canada by Lerner Publishing Group Inc.
241 First Avenue North, Minneapolis, MN 55401 USA
www.lernerbooks.com

Library of Congress Cataloging-in-Publication data is available.

Designed by Verity Clark

Printed in China
1 3 5 7 9 10 8 6 4 2

Into the Wild

For the wandering feet and mind.
~ R V

For Oscar. . . your life was meant
for good friends and great adventures.
~ M A

Into the Wild

Robert Vescio Mel Armstrong

NEW FRONTIER PUBLISHING

NOTES

Roman was a lone wanderer.

If he heard a
grasshopper chirp,

he would follow it everywhere.

Roman craved **wonder** and **surprise** . . .

. . . and wandered **further**.

Roman sought the **hidden**,

the mysterious,

and the **wild**.

There were so many things waiting to be discovered:

living treasures
to see . . .

to touch . . .

and to hear.

But the wild

was too vast

and deep.

Roman looked around, longing to share his discoveries.

And then . . .

. . . an unexpected surprise.

Sometimes when Roman wandered,

he wanted to find one thing.

Other times, Roman
wandered without intending
to find anything at all.

The wild had kept
many secrets . . .

but here was
another wanderer!

Roman crept closer.

He jumped,

climbed,

and tripped.

"Got you!"

They looked at each other and smiled.

Roman found
something interesting.

He found something rare.

He found laughter with someone
special by his side . . .

. . . and no discovery was
ever too small to share.